For Willow, Eliza, Monty, Oliver, Angus, Ben, Albie and Kitty. Let's party! – A.C.

For my sister – R.A.

First
published in paperback
in Great Britain by HarperCollins
Children's Books in 2009
ISBN 13: 978-0-00-717970-1
3 5 7 9 10 8 6 4 2
HarperCollins Children's Books is a
division of HarperCollins Publishers Ltd.
Text copyright © Andy Cutbill 2009
Illustrations copyright © Russell Ayto 2009
The author and illustrator assert the moral right to be
identified as the author and illustrator of the work.

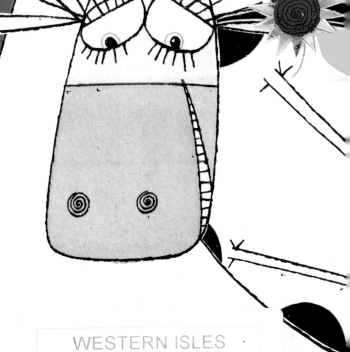

The Best Cow in Show

by Andy Cutbill

illustrated by Russell Ayto

HarperCollins *Children's Books*

One morning Marjorie the cow woke with a jolt.

The farmer's wife was hammering
up a poster in the yard.

Bang! Bang!

BEAUTIFUL
BABY
CONTEST
THIS AFTERNOON B

STRICTLY

"It's a beautiful baby contest!"
read Derek the bull.
"This afternoon before tea. STRICTLY cows only."
"**OOOOOOOOh,**"
said all the lady cows.
They were terribly excited.
So was Marjorie…

Her baby, Daisy, had been a special cow since the very moment she'd hatched from an *egg*!

Mum and baby

"**All my own work**," **said Farmer.**

cow eggs chickens
cow eggs chickens
cow eggs chickens

HOLY COW!

cow eggs chickens c
cow eggs chickens c
cow eggs chickens c
cow eggs chickens c
cow eggs chicken
cow eggs chick
cow eggs chick
cow eggs chickens
cow eggs chickens
cow eggs chickens
cow eggs chickens
cow eggs chickens
cow eggs chickens
cow eggs chickens c
cow eggs chickens c
cow eggs chickens c
cow eggs chickens c
cow eggs chickens c
cow eggs chickens c
cow eggs chickens c
cow eggs chickens c
cow eggs chickens c
cow eggs chickens c
cow eggs

Daisy sleeping yesterday

First hoof print

!" **said a chicken.**

cow eggs chicken
cow eggs chickens
cow eggs chickens
s chickens

All the baby cows started
practising for the contest.

Their mums taught them
to SWISH their tails...

...trot ^{up} and down

...and mooooo delightfully.

Marjorie wanted
to help Daisy.

But Daisy was too busy
with the chickens.

The other cows were
starting to talk.

"DAISY'S VERY
SMALL FOR A COW."

Soon it was time
for the contest to begin.
Derek herded the
spectators into the yard.
"Good luck, Marge!"
called the chickens.

There were **babies**

everywhere!

A nervous hush fell over the barn as the farmer's wife appeared.

Carefully she studied each baby,

checked behind their ears and trotted them around the yard a bit.

Finally she reached Daisy.
"What a fine specimen!" she said.
But as the farmer's wife
bent down, Daisy noticed
something wriggling
in her hat...

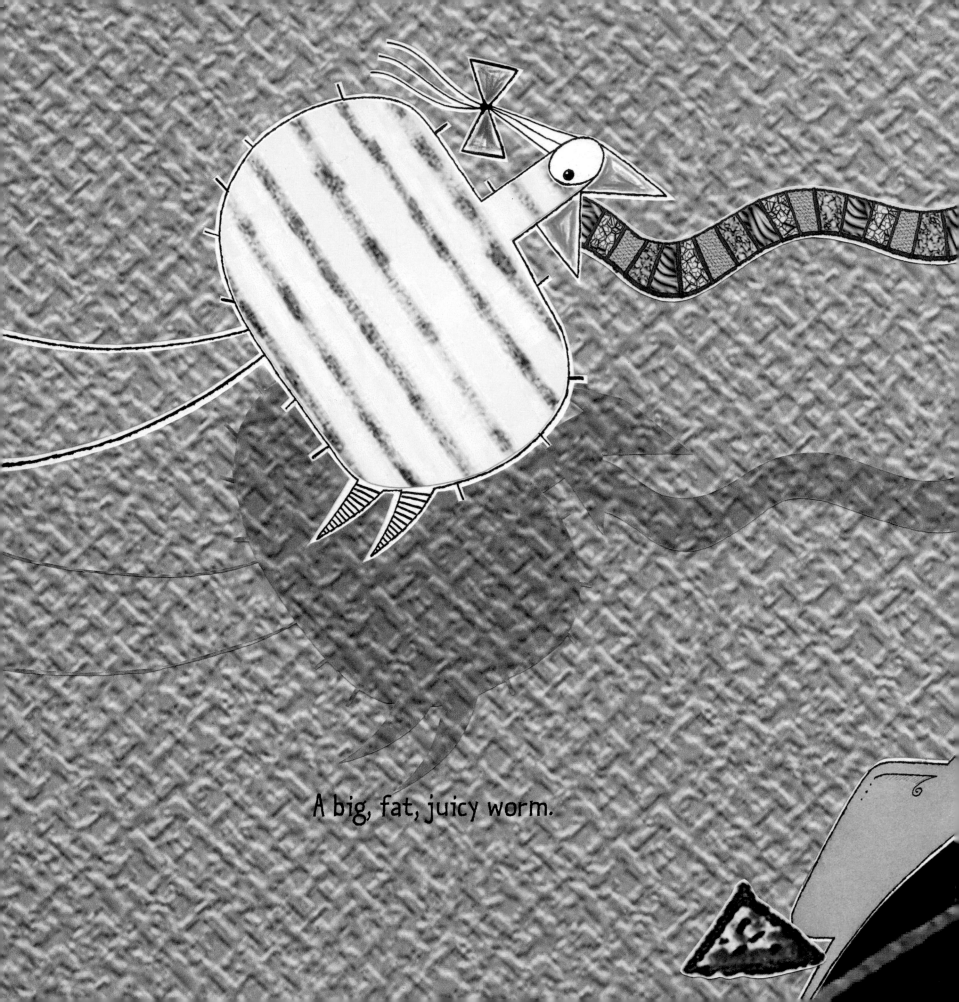

A big, fat, juicy worm.

Gulp!

Daisy swallowed
it whole.

"Well, I never!" whispered the other cows.
Then they began to laugh.
HA HA HA HA HA!

Soon the whole yard
was in hysterics.

Marjorie scooped Daisy into her arms.
"Daisy might not be like your babies," she said,
"but she's mine and I love her!"

Well, you could almost hear a pin drop.

"Glad to hear it,"
said Derek, all of a sudden.

And he promptly
slapped a large rosette
on Marjorie's chest.

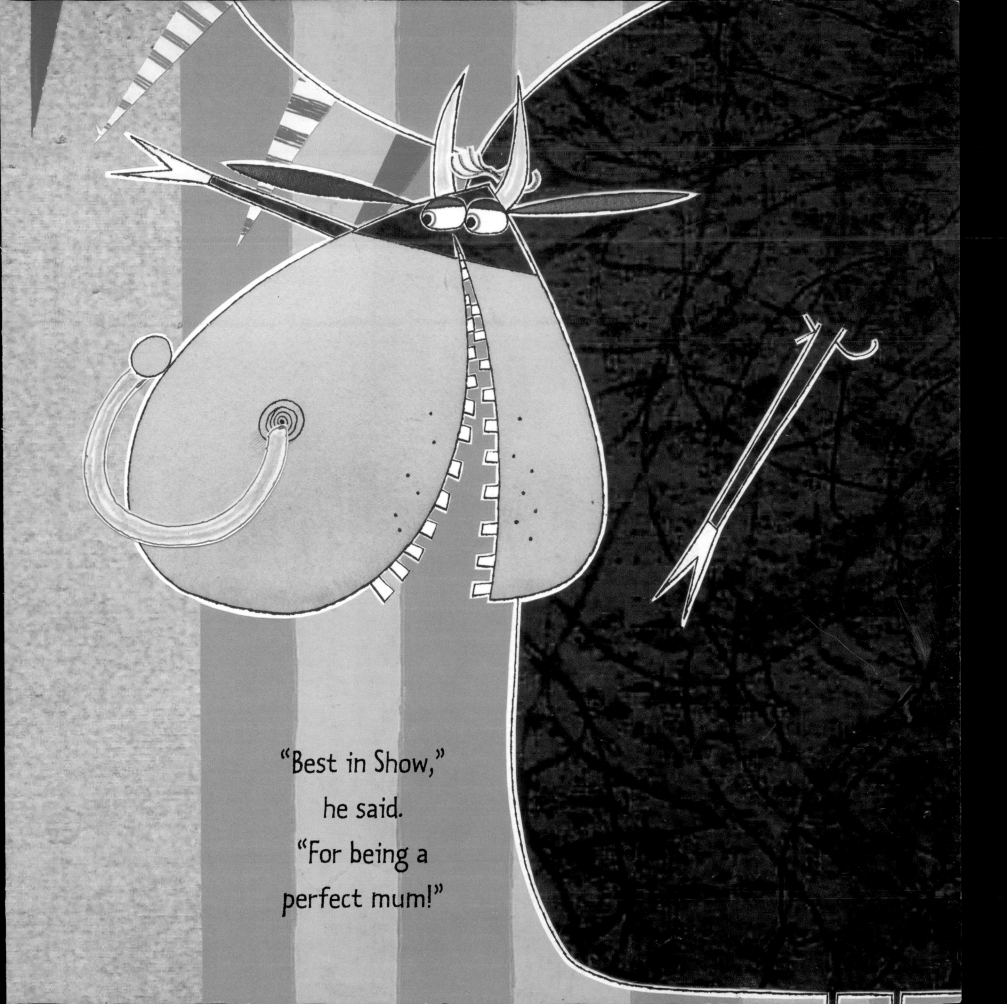

"Best in Show,"
he said.
"For being a
perfect mum!"

Derek gave Marjorie a big, wet kiss.

"Ahhhh," sighed the chickens.
And Marjorie blushed all over.